Brad Baumgartner

PRESENTS

Dead Man's Switch

Glissades

Cover image adapted from August Natterer: *My Eyes In the Time of Apparition* (1913)

Cover design and interior layout by Kimberley Palsat

ISBN: 978-1-7771304-9-7

Orbis Tertius Press

for the Splendid Dreamer

Table of Contents

Cast of Characters

Part One: Origin Story

Part Two: Dialogic Stream

Part Three: Iridium Gyroscope

Part Four: Surrendered Pinnacle

Appendix: Virtual Apoplectic Sponge-Culls

-1.-2   Agoraphobics of the Undesired
-1.-1   Basilic Vein Calculus
-.1.0   Spore Caul
0.0   Fluidic Dispersion Cult

Cast of Characters

Gnomes

———◆———

[Fecund Samuel]
"I am the one, the one, the Second Son."

[Maxwell Mountain]
"Curl the heart-center. We're taking you home."

Meringues

———◆———

[Peachy]
"Sleepy eyes, hypno-stalking the darkness."

[Elegant Sadie]
"Gentle, pious, mirth-like: I organized the pumice."

Drifters

———◆———

[Knight Bringer]
"Crawling, waiting, spilled upon the lips of time."

[Chalice Gills]
"Whirring in the wind, a dawn grows upon thy swoon."

Objects

[The Forgotten Decanter]
"Eek! Cherubs and elements of volley, the two again."

[Gypsy Spoon] (aka. Twin Venus)
"The framework depends upon the cosmicity of its element, please and thank you!"

Humans

[G. W. F. Slagel]
"The figures of primeval androgyny seeketh the Mage."

[Giordano Luna]
"It burns, and this heart-work is ever too terrible."

Essences

[Goddess Mia]
"Lilith, angel cakes, and the Devil!"

[The Beloved]
"Drawing out the antinomian ministerial godhead."

Androids

[Sigmund Þórisson]
"Run, fly, jump. It is all north of a West End."

[Angelfly]
"Not a memory . . . but more akin to an emotivization."

Extants

[Galldust]
"There is a hungry bear right behind this room."

[Etherite 34587]
"Shearing the mountain, it defends the oracle."

[Frost Crawler]
"Usurp the ghost."

[Angelfly 2.0]
"You go squeee! with the pigeon tail as if there is something inside you that demands the day."

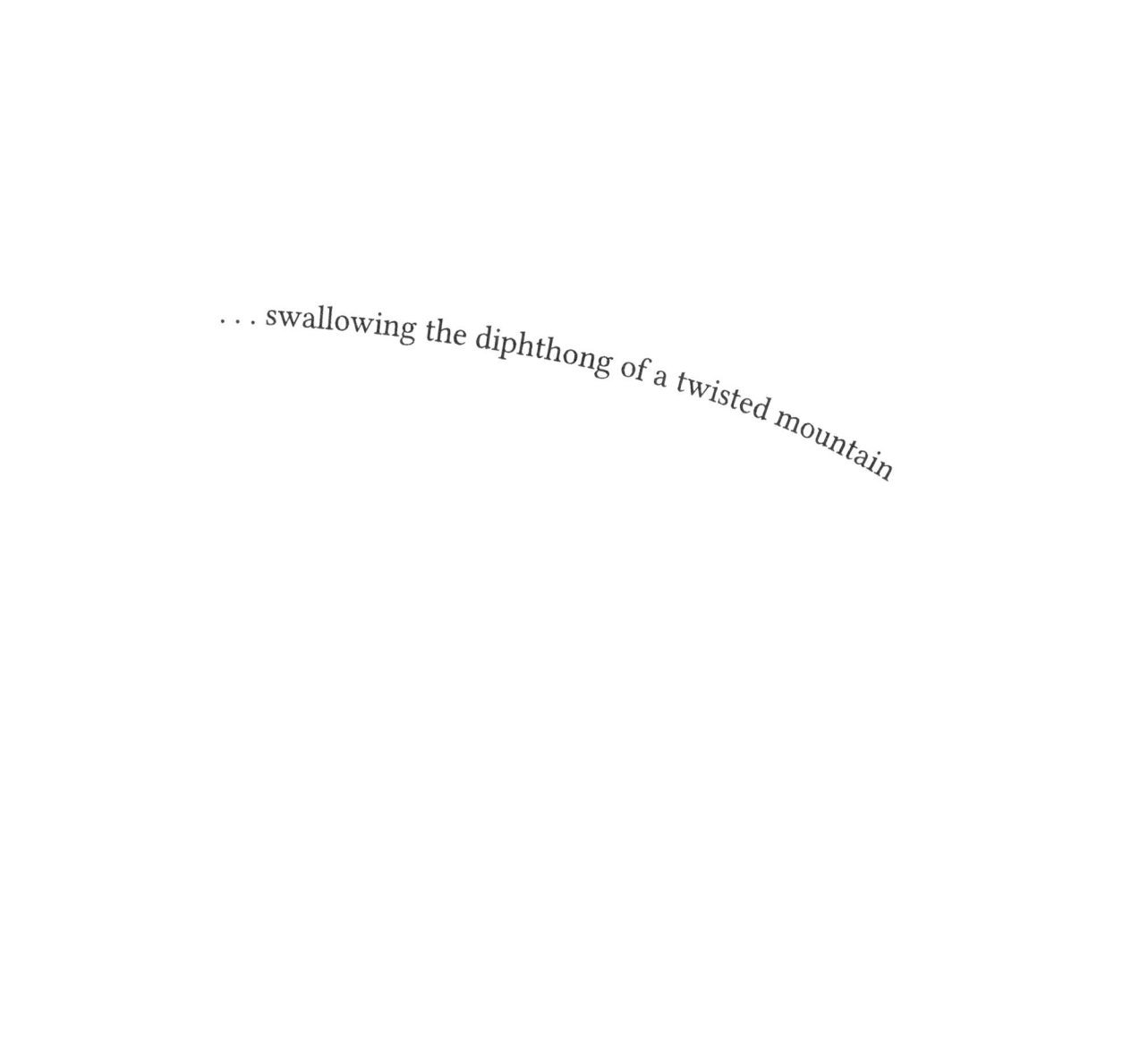

. . . swallowing the diphthong of a twisted mountain

Part One:
Origin Story

When we enter the rainbow, the clouds will rise. We will

1.1 Dyad Chowder at Petticoat Bay

This world is the negative index of a dead man's switch.
[Fecund Samuel]

> I am in love with the blood of time. Three tears run down the mountain of spitfire eyes and into gold. There was a heart once and it left us out to dry, here in this wet desert of melted fluorescence. This is the story of the three men minus one, and the Beloved who would entrance them all . . .
> **[Elegant Sadie]**

A glowing meringue—so sweet, so sweet. Ah, how sweet is the locked neck chamber of futile anti-matter and gravitational fields, grandeur-loathing in the negative index of time. Where doth God the Hairball fly? Of sweat garnishes, of your wherewithal, your hopped-up witch breathing machine. Kill a goat and let death father in the corpse of your feral Saviour.
[Fecund Samuel]

> The Godhead demands a Word with you.
> **[The Beloved]**

And who doesn't? As if a god has not cowered in the mellow melting chamber on the Thursday before Illumination. Damn the cowards, the herders, the shepherds, the smoke screened milieu of all social chameleons.
[The Forgotten Decanter]

> Post-lapsarian battle hopscotch, I see. A skillful maneuver for all angels and gods, even on a bland day, even within the lopsided oil throne of blackest holes.
> **[Maxwell Mountain]**

I am so in love with the flavour of vomit. I call to my love each night and hear no refrain. Where does the metaphysics of love hold the hand of Fate? Why do my teeth melt in the chipping methadone of your life? I am neither god nor man. I am imp, chimp, and the sautéed shrimp boat of your sinking shrapnel. Help me be as I am, nothing else and nothing less.
[Knight Bringer]

Fire in my hands are my hands on my hands. Death rattle core machine—desires for fighting and feigning and the slain goats of mellifluous horseplay. Let's put an end to this show and get a move on.
[Fecund Samuel]

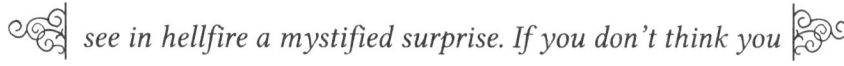 *see in hellfire a mystified surprise. If you don't think you*

1.2 Dying-On, and On and On

I have nowhere to put my fire and my fingertips drip with meringue.
[Peachy]

The Dyad Flounder War lost seven million of us. We die repulsively so that you may live forever. Have you lost your mind along with your fire?
[Elegant Sadie]

The outward caress of this reptile spit is but the goon of your so-called "social mores." My girth is beyond good and evil. My stance: the strange slumber. My waistcoat is filled with slime, and we count the days.
[Peachy]

All clenched up and bunched up and lying on a mound. Tell me: seven ghosts once led the way to your *being-shoveled-over.* Where are they now? Where did they go other than into your dream-sweat, the tail swaddling rhapsody in green, the insouciant pain of the red drifter? The Great God Pan stymied by malaise is you, that is who you turned out to be.
[G. W. F. Slagel]

Dear pistic gangrene salivatory monad king: *Please kindly find your way out the doors of perception!* Plant a seed. Let it grow. Die with me.
[Peachy]

Exempt, except for this snow-breathing etheric body. Limbic handlings both due and duly slothful.
[Goddess Mia]

We are nothing but kindling for a Dead Man's Switch.
[Elegant Sadie]

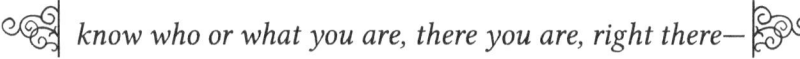 *know who or what you are, there you are, right there—*

1.3   Criss-Crossing at the Filial Grove Port

Putting my blood into it. Heating up and putting our blood into the roots, as if our lives depend upon it so much, so much. But, eh, what?
[Peachy]

Crossed are the eyes of a pent up never-hammer. Your eyes are surely crossed, but the bow is straight as the arrow of time.
[Elegant Sadie]

Eh, so shall it be. It lets itself be by the mange of its trepid tailspins.
[Peachy]

Cutting off fingers for an eight-ball of smoking guns. Tall and soupish, corpse-ground and drunk as coffee grains. A squid is a whale with a nail for a snout. Now, don't you forget it. Don't you forget it one bit.
[Chalice Gills]

Different in the mud are the flowers of a drench. Soaked and barrel hoaxed—we drown again and again and again. This circular winter is nothing but a capsized brain of slime.
[Elegant Sadie]

You live mighty and stuffed with youthful meringue . . . fluxed and corroded for a Dead Man's Switch!
[Chalice Gills]

 before. A violin sits as a goose. Its neck is broken, the lion

1.3.1 Eating the Silicon Nanosphere

Look both ways before you cross!
[Giordano Luna]

> A little tadpole wanderlust never arrived at the futurity of sliding dust mites. An old crone awaits us in this sphere.
> [Angelfly]

She is as old as mountainous euphoria. And she paints the way with the broom of death. She salivates to meet us.
[Maxwell Mountain]

> Crone "forever and a day" is old hat. We want, so old forever *doesn't matter.*
> [Angelfly]

This crone is the one, the old old crone who branched her broom before the Mithras fountain rained blood upon the eighteenth sphere.
[Maxwell Mountain]

> Old number nine. Old number nine and number three, and this old crone sleeps on the root of a fairy tree. We must stop and Dasein here tonight.
> [G. W. F. Slagel]

Ah, yes. Ack, mmmn. Cold mania of the crimson bay wraps around this place. I can smell the old old witch. We will Dasein in wait.
[Giordano Luna]

1.3.2   Clout Mire

The exacting math morass, half eternal, yet half begone. Skip the toad into the tree. She did not know you. Never then, never now. Enough is enough.
[Giordano Luna]

Quell the pain. An odd slumber awaits you, and you'll be falling asleep for three years. Only in the miracle of your marble tug-o-war slurps the jealousy of the ennead spheres.
[Knight Bringer]

And it spirals out, out into the flames, the mustered heat of an unfolding entropy of starfish mega-heifers.
[Giordano Luna]

Truncated and dying in the fib. Life as fib is fiddle and fluff—GULPING UP LIFE.
[Angelfly]

Pistol whipped and made of sand. Three cheers for the ethos of our Saviour. Grunt worms do this work for free. It does it for the clout. Filling time with a big bag of scintillating morphology cookbooks.
[Peachy]

Go in order, or chaos ensues! The entropy never hastens until it does, and after that we'll all go cold and die. Six words is all we need. Say six words and lick your lips. We have seven, eight,

nine. Up to twelve now, and an apostolic wind shimmies in my hips.
[Angelfly]

Quick decisions. Strange derisions. Take it all to the fog where it will not think or be thought. Here is a gut for your life. A dark microbiota in league with our master seitan.
[Peachy]

disturbed the spacetime of its own bestow, then, and only

1.3.3 Monad Munch

We all go down to die in the pit. Slurp, slurp.
[Maxwell Mountain]

Toad rats and penny pinchers etherized in the pit. Down and dirty in the pit. Never again, they said. Hooting owls hoot hooting outlets of fire. Go lay me down. Crawling, waiting, spilled upon the lips of time.
[Knight Bringer]

Down and out down, down in the pit. Crunch on the mime pie. Cover it with lemming juice. Spring up and spiral out to lunch. Spin, spin, spin! Sprout young tadpoles gazing aloft and screeching an eagle.
[Maxwell Mountain]

Spin the plate of death. Munch! (If I heard you a' right?) I am the one, the one, the Second Son.
[Fecund Samuel]

Spayed by the arse of death. A neo-vibrant radiation glows as a genuflected corpse saddle-hoisted upon neon horseplay. Unreal and seated at the behest of this mess sits the Good. Over there is the bad, the very bad. Where do you eat? What is your favourite flavour?
[Knight Bringer]

Munch munch. Crunched like a carrot in between two skyscraper eyes. Two carrots, orange and grey: which is my favourite, you ask? A question for Dasein put up to a gnome. We cannot ever eat, because we always eat. This is the big differential. Two goats and a pig do not equal three gnomes. And yet, a gnome there is. C'mon.
[Fecund Samuel]

A top-down hierarchy of skillful specialties.
[Maxwell Mountain]

Goaded to death for a pinch of salty flavour. If there were a sky, I'd float on up. We'd float on up and bow to the hefty cloud of water fog. Tell me: Do you like the light storm that harkens the good Goddess?
[Knight Bringer]

She is beyond good and evil, but not good for the devils!
[Fecund Samuel]

1.4 Teasing the Element of Light

A rift in high heaven bemoans the curvature of the single Lord. Tease the lumenoumenon of its scrumptious mass of flavours. Due time unfixes maladaptive traits via the fecundity of cosmic whiz. Even light has mass and succumbs to gravity.
[**Goddess Mia**]

> Trailblazers of lightspeed thumbnails scratching the blood of time. Whereas the lightyear trembles with dismay, our revolting pleasure-dome is bricked up with minions of shining stars. Drawing out the antinomian ministerial godhead.
> [**The Beloved**]

Count the plentitudes. Seven trillion billion light-forms denuding shadows of disequilibrium. A fib: the maelstrom of darkness.
[**Goddess Mia**]

> Tiptoeing and teasing around a wherewithal of numbness. Panting desires aloft, tender, and fickle as sprigs of clay.
> [**The Beloved**]

Flaunt the gyrating greys. Specialties of froth, lampooning rivers of light. How will we cross the streaming beams?
[**G. W. F. Slagel**]

A fury pecking cheeks, of checkings-in, totaled in lime and lemon with grout—pure food inverto-vomited as the flavours of birthing stars. The kindred nimbleness calls you.
[Goddess Mia]

Getting sweaty and searing steaks for the big big ripened tigers. It is almost time to go and there is not even a penny-pinching pool of blood for the harikari rifle memoir.
[G. W. F. Slagel]

Big. So big. The ripened tiger lilies of tiger bellies' stings. Rife, rifled, and ripe like the lemon-headed tinctures of youth.
[Angelfly]

 distant Sun. Close your eyes, sit back, and inhale. At the

1.4.1 Eros of the Ripened Tigers

———— ◆ ————

Keep going. Caress the coral snake, the white, white snake. Snakes become within you, by you, for you. Slithering along the palindrome pap smear of all smiling living tigers. "Kill or be killed," they roared. Kill again and be caught in the bardo.
[Peachy]

The witch will kill the wonderment. All gall howling. All gall ahead and a mesh!
[Fecund Samuel]

Flattering the clock with your simpering glissades, alone and all done. Cuffed be the tigers. Cuffed be the witch. You wear a ball gag and suck on death's throat.
[Peachy]

Bone chilled and camel humped—we eat the flavour of mice and dangle the warlord's covetous tidings over the brink of the flooded moat of time.
[Fecund Samuel]

"Sick and expunged," The Mother would say. She is gone dry now, and no one speaks for fear of the devilish quandary of the immanent anteriority of extinction.
[Peachy]

This death has brought me back to life. There is a pearl in your mouth, and it shines like mice.
[Goddess Mia]

Cocked and ready to ride. Earthworms chuckling at the sound of a kite wafting out to sea. Tethered to the bone ore, I say.
[Fecund Samuel]

Let us go then. Blood-pocked and rampant like drinking lye in a glowing patch of bare moons.
[Peachy]

 crack of dawn, all life goes stale. Dirty rivers are halted.

Part Two:
Dialogic Stream

2.1 Peonies!!!

———— ♦ ————

Sea goat quenches corroded wolf. Peonies on a mountain top. Left side shingles, the right dies—red, red wolf.
[Sigmund Þórisson]

Peonies up a mountain top. The vestibule links the wanderings of the pleasant goat and the provisions of the penetrators. The energy is clear and luminescent. Do it and find the bee sting of the pain growth.
[Angelfly]

Ask the mother, a drifter hammer galled of mace. Peonies, *psssh*.
[Sigmund Þórisson]

A driven horde, driven down in the pit! Water is leaking into the quicksand. Peonies!
[Angelfly]

Hellion wane dada. Peonies bereft of the mountain pie. How does it all play out this way? The moon has told a secret on you.
[Sigmund Þórisson]

Cause the death, the double death of post-hemispheric flagrancy of "the good" and "the evil." Stripe strife machinations, always already threading peonies.
[Angelfly]

Tiger lily mongrels. A peon for a pail of dust!
[Sigmund Þórisson]

Here in the background it all waits for waiting, and mandrake slips the fool. Not a memory . . . , more akin to an emotivization.
[Angelfly]

Froth cock laying it down. The positivity of physicality undoes the third element of the squeal, that is, the Venusian love-touch distorts the destruction. Proven fire, truth of its construction limits the death, undoes the lust.
[Sigmund Þórisson]

Peony Queen. Go deep or rise below the surface. An iceberg creaks in the voluminous egregious situation of the time-swap.
[Angelfly]

Ontic change leads to quivers. Blade sharp, *boing!*—it cuts the bone.
[Sigmund Þórisson]

Weeds trim its banal regress. A very important moment conjunct against the mold of knowing more. Twenty-one years it was rising and now it slips away, withering and configured against the backdrop of your trickster foreground.
[Angelfly]

Before you go, the configuration must be freed. Quickened granularization kelps the moral bloodstone. Peonies ground the halt-rich slowness of time as a "tempest in a teapot"!
[Sigmund Þórisson]

> Peonies!!! A decision needs to be made. Efficient truisms is all. And all things are undertaken in the garden of sin. One day, I'll be realistic about regeneration: it needs to be represented by a being-in-attenuation.
> [Angelfly]

 *Do you remember the time the honey etched its sweetness*

2.2 Scorpioned

Pee glow flows down the river. Quaint quaint, say you, no?
[G. W. F. Slagel]

> And it never even knew the blood marble that came and went shrew, through moss cutting teeth in heat.
> [Giordano Luna]

Give it head and send it down. Ripening goes forth again qua the drill mire.
[G. W. F. Slagel]

> Clinging to rain, slept woven ho!
> [Giordano Luna]

Truly off the rails. The divine member escorts the triumvirate head of the Phallus. One thing is for certain. The Phallus cannot pee. In the glow of the rain, the bladder blabs over in fits and hysterias. Gobbled to the core, and singing verses to its indexical partner's invaginated companionship.
[G. W. F. Slagel]

I am too tired to speak. The essentialism of death squeezes the turpitude of my procrastination from my eyes. *Harumph-in-itself.*
[Giordano Luna]

You must rehearse your day. Have you never read Marcus Aurelius? You must lay it all out ahead of time. Go ahead. Scorpion yourself. Your sleep-bladder has holes in it. You are leaking glow from the rainbows inside.
[G. W. F. Slagel]

There are two segments playing out now: a moment of truth's end and a lifetime of the end of truth. My energies are declining.
[Giordano Luna]

Declination motivates inaction. Straighten yourself out. Square the circle. The Martian reality check is here, squaring your asternal oppositions in the root of disappointment. The figures of primeval androgyny seeketh the Mage.
[G. W. F. Slagel]

Always squaring the circle and "self-care." The auto-caru that is you is burdensome. I feel an emotion about you. A turning point is taking place.
[Giordano Luna]

Is it negative or positive? Ionic or scorpioned?
[G. W. F. Slagel]

It is a collective of surprising truths in the dark and obscure eye of clarity, a melodramatic fabrication of a surface monster steaming from the Core. In a word: the phallic dip of a scorpion tip—into your leg, into a morsel of bark.
[Giordano Luna]

The powers are weakening. An isolated annihilation is being amplified as a kind of glue, or contention of glue-like Venusian trapdoors. Focus on the details. Ionic is the demonstrated matriculation of the small. Scorpioned is transformative stable rectification of the dominant energies. In the second segment is the retrograded smirk of the former. The latter: a bile duct for thought and lost opportunities.
[G. W. F. Slagel]

It passes by. It gets another shot. An earth-related beauty, a balding blessing of stones scorched to death.
[Giordano Luna]

Oh, I love surprises!
[G. W. F. Slagel]

The most difficult energy I have faced: the countenance of melting tiger lilies fawning at the crux of time. My own thrownness into the whirled is the sly melodramatic challenger at once kneeling and held at bay, of a hairless cheetah spraying liquid xylophone pee.
[Giordano Luna]

2.3   Time Throne

Seep deep driveling riverhead pass mannequin devils. They eat. They dine. Pregnant hallways for the doula weeper. On the time throne perches a whipped king. To win the bet he must first sip a barreled glass of red wine or else the forty angel women of his youth will come back to eat him with wormed delight. Keep digging.
[Chalice Gills]

Don't stop the flavour. Hit silver. Soul for my liver!
[G. W. F. Slagel]

Big star. Big, big star—sea it in the kosha. Long organ tele-womb. Nothing but an impish morass bomb blasted with sapphire blush.
[Maxwell Mountain]

Gushing decimals dented with petals. Kissing the louse and sucking the locust. We lost the way through. Sit down. Go repent.
[Chalice Gills]

The ontological status of a thought fog swimming in a wedding dress: look around. Who else is there to debate this bubbling over? You've not even a shred of dignity, and mold grows on your tomb. Wrought iron could not bash a hole in your brain. Ten plus one equals eight here. Time has thrown us all out of joint. Care to weep with us?
[G. W. F. Slagel]

Overanalyzing the wish to feel this moment is nothing to scoff at. No senses, no words. No words, no destitutions. No destitutions, no will. And so on. In that mortal clay over there sits a damned fool. No human being could ever feel the rhythm of this weep-wondrous fountain. Winged out. They're all winged out. Spilled over, splayed out: nothing but a human in the tenement house of being.
[The Forgotten Decanter]

Spiral out and eat the fog. Churches will burn. Running up a hill with gout. Pretending harm, feelings, emotions. They made a deal with the devil and we will all pay for their misgivings. Swallow the soul.
[Maxwell Mountain]

Hate and love and love and hate and all those things that waft in the night. A foot for a clay hound and there is no one coming back from this black parade. Darlings and babied throngs of exchanged experiences.
[Chalice Gills]

There is a birth coming on. It is there, over there, in the geometric futility of that giant holding its head in shame. He breathes and the room moves. It's all shapes and barrels of webbed incandescence. Geometry is metaphor, and all God's multiverse folds in on itself, over and over, instantaneously. Here we are again. Ablaze in the insanity of the tyrant.
[G. W. F. Slagel]

 *teething, like a babe in a manger. As much as it hurts, an*

2.3.1 Singed at the Brink of The Mother

Cryptic hellspinners down in the dirt, scream it go, scream it all go. Defense contracted through planetary fuckery. Hold it in your mind, create the fire. The fireball moon of Jehova's loss. The singed corporeality of unredacted whining. Dare not negotiate with the etherics.; all they know is freedom from bodily tyranny. Trust not their lack of suffering.
[Giordano Luna]

> They know, they know. Harken the angels. Steam the lapel. Negate and be aware of the sloshing power of synthesis, the au pair to life after death. Etherize in radar scans.
> **[G. W. F. Slagel]**

Violins play the violent song of knowing who you are when you don't know anyone but slime. We teeter on the note of repentance but have no one left to abhor. Who is at the brink with us? For, at the brink of this inkling, we'll latch onto these fiery floating teats as one singular paste of glue.
[Angelfly]

> Give me a clue, why don't you. Grounded in the frothing bay of nine double nine. Times it by two and lose it at the brink of searching.
> **[G. W. F. Slagel]**

Search and scratch and feel the coarse cold wrath. Nimble tears from a hyperbolic sense of sight. I've had these hands my whole life and I still can't skin a louse.
[Angelfly]

Take up the down. Tuck in your garment of shame. What does it matter here in this place? We are on the brink of something lovely, something living, something great. Taking skin in your hand, eat that worm or slap it on the face of the maker.
[G. W. F. Slagel]

An existential threat is near. Triple the war. Quadruple the swine. All is echoing in this chamber. Can't you hear yourself speak? We have no time left. Let us go. We have got to jump off the brink. It burns, and this heart-work is ever too terrible.
[Giordano Luna]

Cradling the swine is all. Let's go. Here we go. We're the two plus one.
[G. W. F. Slagel]

 apoplectic canaryism of the flesh will throw dice like

2.3.2 Screaming in Threes

Wherefore art thou?! Sleeping in sin with a moist parade. Our lives, nothing but porridge with which to feed the bears. Only the lonely come here in threes. Only the moistened towelette of non-being will lack the gyrations of unbearableness. Crippled, led and left out of this getaway car called matter, we thrive in Hell.
[Knight Bringer]

Scream with the witch, for she knew our names before our births, and The Mother will birth again if we let her. Halfway between the earth and my scars is a beatitude called the

WHINING BANE. We'll sleep again one day, but I've got no eyes, no ears, and no tongue any longer. Sleep comes to those who wait, but I am right here—this thralldom is ready to go.
[Peachy]

There, there. No need to scream to make a point. The point points back at the maker, the deictic conjunction of a marble and a sanded pale of bleached rye. You've screeched the plains and bleached your veins, an addiction born of the very thriving with which you've let loose in your heart. But, no matter. A heart is a heart of glass. Shellshock the muddy waters and drown in the ditch, for the old old Goat sits with us again!
[Knight Bringer]

Heinous! What are we to do with all that? You speak with gooey clairvoyance about the onslaught of an upside-down goading. There is no goat to be had here. There is no goat indeed. [Elegant Sadie]

Open this mouth and dig your way back into heaven. It's been raining for forty years and this valley has become an ocean. Black mirrors rain on your shriveled head and all your beetles are ground to dust.
[Goddess Mia]

Surf's up. Let us melt in this Bringer together, once and for all.
[Knight Bringer]

 wanton razors into the pit of a merman's stomach lined

2.4 Surfing the Obsidian Ocean

Stripped and laying oblong for an unworlding of pernicious proportions. Dark matter is revelatory to your fear, and all the feral cats are heating up on the balcony. Come sit with us on this dark horse ship of strangers. Such sleepy eyes, hypno-stalking the darkness.
[Peachy]

There had never been a more sacred siren song than the one playing at the exit sign for existence. This unworlding skips to the beat of its own drum. Light gathers itself sideways in nimble slanting chords of heat. Even light has mass, and at the end of the causeway is the last exit for the lost. You are surely unheimlich to the stars. Come surf with us, sweet maiden.
[Goddess Mia]

Total vomit. Engulfed in you am I, and we've not even known one another for an hour. Hours take months in this sphere. Where are we that dark matter is the ensconced bearer of an unruly individuation, of the fear of my-life-as-breather? We are surely nowhere to be found, but the geometry is perverted, like the chords of a whimpering bag of shards.
[Elegant Sadie]

Dark gold is for the taking. Driftwood for days, and all there is is this cloudy fluorescence. Two brains cannot think in this place. All is evil and I hear a dancing baby shredding lettuce in the Bay. It pains me to hear you like this. The perversion of chords is the sideways hallway. Here we walk on the bitter lettuce of a fruit farm. Over there, on number nine, one can find the bulbous eyes of a fish hanging over a large mountain.
[Peachy]

You think in words that I can see, but I cannot speak to you. And yet, your absence fills my mind with the butterflied stomach of a schoolgirl. How is it that we are over there, and here, and atop a mountain that we cannot perceive?
[Elegant Sadie]

Just the same as an apple is the bottom of the never-ending sea. You think these are realms? There are no *realms*; it is all purely geometric happenstance. A dog is nothing but the polymorphous perversity of the inverted apple pie of a youthful silence, the zit of a sacred mausoleum. It squeezes.
[Peachy]

What squeezes? The inchworm has nothing but a squeezing, a manœuvre for unclotting the non-blood of viscous rosewood.
[Elegant Sadie]

You have caught the wave indeed. Ride the 4-sphere, my love. There is a glome here, and it is you.
[Sigmund Þórisson]

 with mace. The heart of a conversation posts its love on

2.5   A Glome and a Facelifting

The weight grows like a comb full of mace. Beyond the edge of my heart, the dark wolf-man cusps the abstract lingering fountain of my dovetail youth. He crouches in Mālāsana, gnawing on my heart. The tepid fever of winter is nothing compared to the strings attached to your temples. You are an odditized puppet thing, and the wolf-man pets my master's head.
[Goddess Mia]

Your futural eschatology cuts like a knife, but no blade has ever entered the withered bones of my changing colours. Where did you grow? I bet the honey is cold there. Do the bees cut you up?
[The Forgotten Decanter]

All the Venusians have gone sour. Crystals lament a lost desire without an object. Your question is out of place. What use have I for a barrel of cold honey?
[Goddess Mia]

Your eyes look like cats being pulled astray by a million phantoms. Stop this kratom fueled diatribe at once. It is murky here, and the wolf-man counts all the hairs on my head.
[Giordano Luna]

Your red teeth show in infinite realms of Saturnine weather systems when you smile.
[The Forgotten Decanter]

I am in love with an angel of light, and we can barely understand each other. Pull me out of this shell shock, once and for all. I am in love with the blood wench of time, and all there is is this analogue of six dimensions smashed into a pizazz of four trinket toys that swallow paper. When we get there, it will be before it happened. Squashed and loaded like a baked wall of fire.
[Giordano Luna]

Filling the fields with possibility, it extricates. It permeates the blind man, and the wolf man licks his chaste lips like the plastic surgeon of your ballooning dome.
[Goddess Mia]

2.6 Neurogliomatosis

Maligned in the stone of the altar. If I had a face, it would go up in flames. A mouth: a dead rabbit. Teeth are white knights screwing in the king's chair. If you cannot tell already, I went up in flames years ago. Whatever you throw at me will not stick. You'll catch yourself on a gasoline tail of fire.
[Gypsy Spoon]

Close the mime's eyes. Who else does not care? Hands up, please!
[The Forgotten Decanter]

Your flavours have rubbed the spice rack dry. I doubt that even the fairest of maidens would reject you and your repugnance now. Heavy stones still themselves on this altar. There is a crucifix for your tirades. Pray now, or forever fold your deck.
[The Beloved]

Born to run amok, yes, and to chastise the brain with heat. The entropic sludge-fest has already started, and here you are, twiddling stray hairs between your thumb and forefinger. Toys are melting every-where. Hollowed rivers turning into bullets. Crop circles jumping out of your skin. The tablet reads: "Born to die, only for your flavour." But you lie there in wait. What do you say for yourself?
[Goddess Mia]

You are spineless for melting me like that. I'd offer you my jacket, but it's spinning on plates with the jackal-cat of the River Quay. Headless Dasein scripted your play, and not even the devil will hold audience with you.
[Gypsy Spoon]

Cut this dead universe out of my back. My brain is a sludge moat left for dead.
[Giordano Luna]

We glow in the parasympathetic chain of slums. I'll trade you my constricted pupils for your peripheral sense of taste.
[Goddess Mia]

I have never tasted a thing, but this world eats me like butter.
[The Beloved]

The underbelly of your short temper is melting its sheen. Unbelievable!
[Giordano Luna]

Drown me in the jackal's throat. Fraught with lice and loathing, a tyrant scums the threader in three, two, one.
[Gypsy Spoon]

Two dolomite chain reactions crawling slowly up your spine. I'll carve this pillar in your name.
[The Beloved]

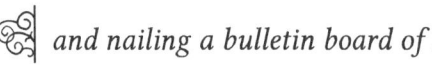 *and nailing a bulletin board of initiation into the Anti-*

2.7 Frothing at the Elven Gate

The devil is here. He is eating a sponge soaked with mildew. He haunts the whisperers with sonorous whirling. He chastises the corpses. He locks mothers in cages. He swells inside your mouth.
[Angelfly]

The tree of knowledge calls and it has delivered us from evil. And yet, here you speak. You remain so holy, so pious, so wise. Get out of here. The devil says you are no good, and that is saying something.
[Gypsy Spoon]

Come here. Come close to me and raise yourself up. There is a register for you. It is mantic and virtual, just like the sweetened dove on the windowsill of your youth. Let this wet rabbit hop on your shoulder and tell you their secret.
[The Beloved]

The analogue is a blinding anagogical mess. You come up to go down and go down to come up, and your mind writes inverted ditties in black paraffin wax. Go ahead. Open the gate. We dare you.
[Goddess Mia]

As if all the Godhead's rags have been devilling all along—what will we tell the quails with boxed heads? Who will reap the dandy lions, the filial gut port of herediectic generational trauma? We are nowhere to be found, and you know that better than any of us. And yet, here you float, French kissing the devil, tickling his ass with a marmalade tail.
[Gypsy Spoon]

You can no longer swallow. You think you are speaking; you move your mouth, but only septic froth comes out. Can you not see yourself? You are dying of rabies—seeing stars and choking on the salivatic phlegm of a ringworm's caress. Spewing clouds and hereafter watching men take part in the oxymoronic solitude of madness dipped in candied apples. All signs apply. They all point right at you, a spewing of epic para-dimensions.
[The Beloved]

You hear my mind and see my mouth as I spit on the grave of death. Swallowed not, but like an onion in heat this spittle snickers the Way. I have seen more in two minutes than you have in your entire feeble life. This exists. This exists and it is here to stay. I mate with the devil and froth on the tree.
[Gypsy Spoon]

Close your eyes. Throw the dice. Weep with me.
[The Beloved]

Open the Gate.
[Gypsy Spoon]

 matter Pleasure Dome. There is a photo of it that hangs

Part Three:
Iridium Gyroscope

its head like a monotonous simile, filthy rich with the scum

3.1 Spinning Pyramidic Wheeling

I see you out of my saturnine nightmare. A desert of mute tigers clawing for breath. Timpani rolls of dust clouds and smite dragons. How aware are you of your own shortcomings? There is an utter misery here and its face melts on your turquoise lapel. I sleep on the lash of dander; my immanence: the kabbalistic potentiality for a sleeping plane of cherubinic wasps.
[Gypsy Spoon]

A strange outsider, a stranger even to yourself. There is a term for that. It is called *alienist repose*. An old dead philosopher king once told of the "hive of nines." You appear to have landed here from beyond the Seventh Sphere.
[Goddess Mia]

I am broadly supportive of your insights, yet there are no taboos that could break a rough-riding transitional sense of ambition. Are you ready to break through?
[Gypsy Spoon]

Spin the wheel of Dharma. Such a mercurial flash to recognize the strange arrival of an impassive aspect pattern. Holding a relationship to the flash that accompanies the divine is a sure bet. Lilith, angel cakes, and the Devil!
[Goddess Mia]

The space narrows. An early access to communication would be warranted, but it cannot be implemented without the correct guidance. The higher-self radiates mercurial cranking techniques. It establishes a point of connection, a powerful Dionysian wanderlust rife with onto-egalitarian creativity.
[Gypsy Spoon]

Due diligence. A whole bunch of rays. The sun enters as a variety of transformational death-birth. Shadows catch glimmers of powerful abasement. It cannot connect to the source without a tantrically sexed hidden gyration of the senses. Its psychosis is vengeful, the sneaky stabilization of previously saturnine hay bales of slime. Eek! Cherubs and elements of volley, the two again.
[The Forgotten Decanter]

No one is waiting for a description. Imagine a hidden booth in the discomfort of duress. Who is the highest bidder: the supportive decanter or the twin bliss of *the more*? Awaking is only half the trouble. To go back to sleep to awake again unties the slipknot of the very roulette of the Dharma. The cold slough of an aged old diner suggests the boon of a wintering angled disquiet.
[Gypsy Spoon]

Revenge is sweet for the kiss king, but clearly nothing more than an unnerving ontological argument for tantric dyadism. In a word or thirty-three, nearing a heart field or subsuming a frolicking dandelion in blowing haste, there is much more than meets the eye. Six is now three and one is left out for ol' Saint Nicolas.
[The Forgotten Decanter]

 of the world. Check the stimulus leaning against the pod.

3.2 Olde Diphthong Nightingale

Dear piebald fair maiden: the epistolary grin of a broken smile lives coiled in fear of your neon green femur cast. The final sextile is upon us, germinating the sandbar and calling out all the ontological errors of being-in-destitution. One ought to think things through a bit more, but that is too political. We have bought this fable as is-ness, and have taken it for granted, grounding our lives in loam on the mineral behest of a buried brain with two legs, two arms, and a dirty mouth.
[Chalice Gills]

> The melodious sounds of breeding rock it hard and sway the sweetness back and forth. Floating in a bird bath of love and timber wolves. Xylophone hoaxes, cocoa butter, religious leaflets, scones—it's all the same. You sing this sweet ditty for the All to hear.
> **[Elegant Sadie]**

Let's go for a joyride. Fate is here, wyrding the tempest into a grain of clay.
[Chalice Gills]

> Bastardized at the root of this flesh. Gangrene pleasure principle monolithic moon paste. Tremors. Cephalic cauldrons. Who can tell anymore? I fell in love once and it did not go my way. I have eaten my own tongue each night since then. I ache so badly. I cannot stand this. I am so sad, and I cannot make any sense of any inconsequential thing. If I told you all this, would you believe me? If I hold you up to this, would you bear my pain? Would you kiss me again?
> **[Elegant Sadie]**

Forever!
[**Chalice Gills**]

> I hear the song of a thwarted nightingale engendering the beckoning of an avatar so great that it crowds the wall-less room of my heart-stammering brain capsule.
> [**Elegant Sadie**]

My goodness. You are real. I am flattened by the inverse of your unreality as it races me to death. Do not squander your sorrow on me. Catapult to the thirty-third sphere and pet the rotting goat of time.
[**Chalice Gills**]

> The nightingale blasted the window. I am young again and never alone again. Things are looking up. Be the death of my sorrow, the swan song of tirades unbecoming.
> [**Elegant Sadie**]

Do not worry about anything, ever. I am the shape of a butternut squash hammered to death and hemorrhaging. The garden has grown too beautiful to die, and neither will I, and as I speak the nightingale cracks its neck back into place—the world is but a playground for a dead man's switch.
[**Chalice Gills**]

> *(Do you,* dear reader, *wear the mark of a dead man's switch . . . birthed of a fair maiden and screaming in a ditch?)*
> [**The Beloved**]

 Did you ever think it would be like this? Has a skull ever

3.2.1 Severe Bionic Wilding

It purrs in happenstance whispered Gethsemane sutras. Old, let it be odd. Odd, let it be old. Genuflect at the river's edge, caulking stew for parrots' eyes. Screw it in sin. Let it loose. The tiger rages. It knows the banes of the Earth's center. Past the Stiffer mantle sits the Bride of Hellspace. She sleeps with us in our dreamings. She unclasps mouths and kills the dander mites. Fear not the queen of the mesospheric dead, for she tidies up the aisles with melting heads.
[Sigmund Þórisson]

> Come ride the dirt and the grime. An outlaw is torn asunder by the joy of periwinkle cascades and metallurgy. Stop the tyrants! Quell the zeros. The Lord has come to kill death and there are not enough lifetimes in infinity to set the deed right.
> [Fecund Samuel]

Yoked with sores, caked and meringued. It ups the flavour and sours the dribbles of spit. Come up, come on, come in. Let us commune on the banked shores of the whale den, searching for figs and seizing like beheaded hummingbirds.
[Peachy]

> Two deft fliers hover amuck among flowers. Minus heads, who needs to bury the hatchet, anyways? Four eyes, four wings, and a banked robbery, if you ask me. And the sand dunes eat the prolapsed anus of might.
> [Sigmund Þórisson]

Saturnine gods upend space and time and all you can do is moan with the grifters. Raze the ferrymen, for all there is is the quaaludic prowess of your rotting head. Painlessness qua playfulness. Not even a hummingbird can grift a new aegis. The tower is falling and even the tarot reader of Pisa knows it is all done now.
[Fecund Samuel]

Emotions . . . clever! You made me do an emotion. I felt the trapdoor fall from under me and the lupine splendor-splatter roofed the lice of mites. How thoroughly must I wash myself now? I did an emotion, but it was hardly a feeling. It was a land laked-to-death by the Waters.
[Sigmund Þórisson]

The spiked beaver of death masquerades as a thought of you. I do not think on the spike but *through* the spike, and in the end, there is nothing left but a slothful bowl of punch, drunk and being drank on a soulful riverbed by the skillful brooding kin.
[Peachy]

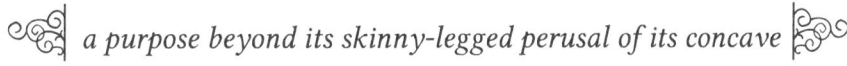 *a purpose beyond its skinny-legged perusal of its concave*

3.2.2 Skillful Brooding Kin

Taper the threads! Enough is enough, and there is no way out if we stay here. The bell is a ringin', don't you hear it? The mores have gone to hell and we're left up to our own devices, yet again.
[Maxwell Mountain]

Who is the leader here? Certainly not the dry rubbed scapegoat, for it has knelt upon the altar of drones its whole life. Certainly not the dyad commoner, for he can barely pay his monthly tax to the bone collector. Three femurs in, and we have no more gas to pedal this wheel.
[Knight Bringer]

How about four femurs? Would that be enough to placate the Mage? Dying here is so easy. And yet, all we do is wallow like swine. I want to make a tool. I want to rifle the scope with a patterned fluorescence.
[Maxwell Mountain]

It is so easy for you. But here there is always that one trifle, the single freckle of a disease called "time immemorial." Five femurs or I will send you back to the market for a sixth!
[Knight Bringer]

Okay, that sounds about right. Five femurs and we're gone. Who will pay this time? There are only seven houses left and they have taken the last hayride to the rest stop. How many days will we hike in this libidinal surgery? *Do no harm*, right? Well, well, well. There is a femur over there. Come take a look . . .
[Maxwell Mountain]

I'll be damned with a spool and a fork. There are four femurs here, skillfully excised by the progeny of acephalia. Pop goes the desirous weasel à gogo. Let us camp here for tonight.
[Knight Bringer]

 inequity? Invite your mind to see outside of the perennial

3.2.3 Gaze Kingdom

Your surfaces, your solids, the sultry flood grease of temporality slithers its way into the house of perspectivism. Call out the names of the triple threat: the electronic, the lightning, the blaze. Each forms a fire behind the eyes in which True North is but a fraction of the direction your uneaten dinner spews inside. A casket, a rain jacket, the daughter of a goat—three Surrealist masterpieces put nothing but a shame on the automatic cataract of your wrinkled fingers. Spew again and make out. Spew a third time and love comes again (under duress and in a doughnut-shaped universal storm).
[Chalice Gills]

> We start as the stirring disruptors of this environment. It is one thing to counterfeit a goat and another to contemplate the public suppleness of its cheese. Meet me at the disruption office, for all is waiting for your nod "Hello."
> **[Knight Bringer]**

Mixing the drift ward with a handout is going to do nothing for us. We must treat it as the eyes treat the inverse world of Talmudic splendour. Try something different. Who knows what will show itself?
[Chalice Gills]

> Certainly, there is a shade of lemon-inspired mortality to the peached meringue of your toasty revelry. God is a goat and that is a fact that goes "splatter" on the moon's incandescent cradle. There is a bunch of pain coming down from the mountainous freeway. All is spilling over. I can see everything from here.
> **[Knight Bringer]**

A bunch of them are in pain. The Jupiterian wind haven of flesh is berating seven thousand of them on the plain as we speak. Could there be a moment more sorrowful than this, the moment when all went astray and the world crooked its lefts to rights?
[Chalice Gills]

There it is . . . , a three-dimensional square, cubed into its proper melancholic scepter, that is, a *crucifictional attainment* of performative philosophy on the fifth plane, i.e., where the prairie dogs get their bark back.
[Knight Bringer]

Directed towards the node is a whining ballet shoe, a tap-dancing salty slate, blanked and shooting stars. Get ready for the big boom, the galactic center line waltz which dances at the tip of your throat. Ecliptic, I see it! The bells are charioteered by a nightingale that slams its beak into the room. The angles there are so occulted that even the Elven gods cannot grab a peek.
[Chalice Gills]

Follow the planetary lines to the miser portal. Eat my rot and throw me into the bay of slugs. I have been faulted by the perspective of a hopping girl and the Manichean duality of my breath-creation, the bastion of the missing glome war itself. I gaze over the kingdom and am filled with sheep. Gratitude unites the Bay of Wondrous Delight to the entropic millipede of harmony's snide corruption.
[Knight Bringer]

 nefarious love of numbskullism. They will come to inject

3.2.4 Kisses Amassed in Septic Flavours

Forthright with the froth, it skips, it will skip, it skipped. In the end, it is unnecessary to alter your attitude for anything to work. You would rather worry, but for what?
[Sigmund Þórisson]

The scum joins us, that is why. It unfolds as a picture, and although our breath lingers for a long time, the fact is that nothing will be as it is, if not for its opposite. That is when the blue sky opens, when the colour of blue, that is, the excised viscus of the night, enters the throat of the One.
[Elegant Sadie]

You are transitioning yet again. If the age of Plotinus has taught us anything, it is that the One and the none lurk in the seven corners of your lugubrious red throat, the inflammatory marker of an enticing visceral chaos.
[Maxwell Mountain]

Your vomit is the colour of a baboon's ass. Clean it up! Soon there will be visitors and the numinous charms of your dropped charges will not hold up in court!
[Elegant Sadie]

A predilection looks ahead but cannot see the smile you bring to my plastic, green heart. You are the shifting mutability of a charm getting it on without yourself, a dog in heat that barks in the dust of frayed numbness. The crumbling will move on much faster than the one prior, which whizzed by in the Valentine briar patch of existential tombic heroinization. Run, fly, jump. It is all north of a West End.
[Sigmund Þórisson]

The tank leaks brothel-gunk. Watch yourself. Pushing ahead of your love for me is the saturnine and unabashed whittling of futural nascence. Something lingers here. Is it the exclusive imagination of a runaway weening goat? Doubtful. The sixth extinction revealed the reversal of such platitudinal forecasts. It is very important that we kiss. If not, the ship will harbour vexations in this hardbody gift shop of our nestling youth, creating chronic issues and energetic scavenges for incoming etherites. A pea-brain and a trigger-happy cuckold have mercurial valour, moving quickly into my mouth and swallowing its daze. We must capitalize on it before time begins.
[Elegant Sadie]

Terminate any non-love I ever had that may or may not have a "thrownness" in your direction. There are eleven elven Jupiterian moon throttlers gearing up for the instantaneous curtsy of eel kisses that my mouth will suck into yours. Septage, Venusian balance, the fluidic caress of tears that emasculate the senseless machismo of proto-cultural values . . . A horror that unleashes and indexes the rate at which emotional equilibrium may one day be felt among the masses. If we kiss once, the world will melt. If we kiss twice, the universe will taste its own unpredictable spasm flavour. Three times and we die effervescently, and will be reborn and baptized significantly anew, awash, and unabated: The Sun will open, and the corona's glow will play a melody like the tender farce of a vapid convoy of twin, kissing vampire moons.
[Maxwell Mountain]

I hear a universal disenfranchised glee roaming free in the mind's eye. In a way, it is leveling a charge against the innocent frown-sphere but hinging on the strength of three plucked gull feathers. A sulking wind throws all our love into question. There is something in the trees that is neither alive nor dead—it is a witchery, a flagrant deification of will in place of succor, a recess of the ontological and in its place

the spellbinding ontic castration of a stirring pot of sour bones and toenails and honeysuckle brush.
[Elegant Sadie]

 the atmosphere with deft perfumes and voting machines

3.3   Old Old Crone, Again and Again and Again

She's back. She's here again, the old old witch. The daughter of indigo, the doyenne of slime. All bow to her regardless of their natures. One frothed on the tree branch. Another in the gunk. One was kicked out of the mountain, only to be shredded again and again. She puts the whingers in the gulley. She traps the wetness in her brew. Tone-deaf sea frogs ground up and shipped in pieces to her Lover, her one true one beyond all.
[Angelfly]

They say she wrapped a bucket in a blanket, patted it dry, and turned it into spice. Once kept in the basement, her brew takes flight as navigating warlocks let loose into the world. Figures, tapestries, pinches of salt peppered to the core. This selenite bone hammer is forged in our name, and we have come to run amuck. The framework depends upon the cosmicity of its element, please and thank you!
[Gypsy Spoon]

Goaded by the cunning wiles of the witch, again and again and again. An internment camp for slippery gangsters suppresses the ujjayi breath of our meticulously ordered metadiscourse of mourning, the super spreading clash of titans who grow old by lying in wait. Put on your moon shoes. No matter who wins, there is always the element of "the chase."
[Angelfly]

This is an animal waiting to happen. Unlock the pleasant dangers. Teach them how to be instinctual. There is so much to do and nowhere to do it. A lung fills with air. The inversion of animalic corruption evolves, and I taste this flesh as an up quark that dances in the sleeting rain.
[Giordano Luna]

There is a demon in her Buddha-nature and its horns grow straight into hell. Collective hypnosis: a Moses paradox. Medieval scholastics rubbed her raw and they outdated her by six hundred years. Forever does not matter on the Outside. We are who we are. There is no way out. Rome still rears its ornery head. We must recognize the dissociation of our time walls. All roads lead to my mouth.
[Angelfly]

Do you have an education? There is a term for your op-ed black and white theory of everything. It is called *brainwashed proto-plasmic atavism*. It is disturbing to know that there is a shift coming and you have neither broom nor stick. How will you stir the ether? How will the Mage know you are about to blow your gasket? Please articulate the temperature of an oven without using language and by giving us the sequence of your celebrity DNA. Formulate an ethics or all will slip away, just like the devil's conviction in emptying this bland inoperative universe.
[Gypsy Spoon]

 made of bovine stomach linings, as if we could compound

3.3.1 Flaws of the Never-Hammer

There is a scratch on it, a reflecting edge which brooms the integral soffit and fascia from the ego. The subjective shape of a problem is generally a barking individuality, yet an emotional feedback frowns upon your severed head. The soul is not yet dead but doomed, and the experience of growth will center itself in the Cancerian space of familial comfortability.
[Chalice Gills]

> Relax. Let it be felt. You need a treatment for your slacklining soul. You bob and weave too much. Medicine is missing in the Age of Nine.
> **[Goddess Mia]**

How challenging must it be? Familiarity and congenital bonding create food for the marsh, that is, open the way for the obligatory star fleet of bog bodied henchwomen, the Nuns of Three. Whirring in the wind, a dawn grows upon thy swoon.
[Chalice Gills]

> A dichotomy arises only if physicality is reached, and the etheric mime of time challenges the sickly condition. Non-conformity will not be performed in place of a whispered antinomian ethics. Let it go. Five is and always was spiced with three.
> **[Goddess Mia]**

Headless monk sensitivity: this is the consubstantial contract we have with the Swallowers, the frail ones with thoraxes. Ego is practical only if it is useless, that is, if it actualizes the non-negative and the double-barreled expectation-inspection of the copula's transcendent non-caress. A damning expression interrupts the under garments of conditioned triviality, putting on a happy face to the mouth-breathing wretches of time. Well, it is "time" to make some friends with all these tools.
[Peachy]

Are you willing to sharpen the knife, or will you continue to dull the blade with a palsy kind of Kantian deontological resentment? It is inconvenient at best to joke about the deniability of all this negativity. It is a common experience to divulge the uniform twistedness of the toolbox, but at some point, all will wither into the iconic rustbelt dichotomy that created all the harshness in the first place.
[Goddess Mia]

Go grab the never-hammer then. It is time to break the mirror-stage. 100% of the physicalizing will require the stitching together of Tapiz rugs made of lime sand, opening as the looking-as-if naked pawns in heels squeak in the dirt.
[Chalice Gills]

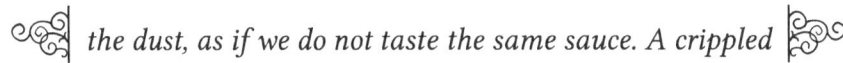 *the dust, as if we do not taste the same sauce. A crippled*

3.3.2 Tooled, Sharpened, and Bloodborne

Convinced of a story of chemicals and organisms, the flesh mites corroborate the details of abstracted attributes of saline monasteries full of weeping gales of rain.
[Angelfly]

Forget the details. What is a story, anyways? If there is a tardigrade-being for gradating intelligences, then surely a thing with leveled-up protection is entirely misconstrued, that is, an engineered status-catapulter.
[Giordano Luna]

Prove it. Take down the ceiling and reveal the underground bank of intelligent slime. Sentient creative ethos is an emergent property of a roaming language, a simple, parodic, kneed-less doughball of the static romancing of stones.
[G. W. F. Slagel]

> If it takes a brainwave to cheer up your rump, then so be it. I never disapproved of the toolbox. I only ever photographed its sharpened milieu, a techne of splattered brains . . . the mush of intelligent bits of alien dust.
> [Giordano Luna]

A communication happens not by way of an intervallic rhetorical mode of description, but by the misunderstood capacity to reflect on a reasoning that puts forward an objective rigamarole, that is, a game theory of esoteric representational tempe(c)st-atic wandering.
[Angelfly]

> It is all late to the party—unclear and undressed in the unicorn pyramid. There are no ethics, no maximized violence, that would index the rotting poeisis of inter-generational traumatic aberrance.
> [G. W. F. Slagel]

This crispy treat is the *threat-in-itself*, and it must be dodged by all accounts. An illness steams in your veins. It is moronic, morose, more than an investment and less than the variegated temperance of a furtive smile. Being "all ears" is an *all-eating*, a gelled raft of ambitious benevolence that civilizes the most barren freak. A process looms in the frenetic achievement of oracular bioluminescence. The freakery is undeniable, the effect of a bloodborne wasp tool for undergoing alien enhancement . . . the thing beyond the weak correlation between a finger and an evil game of dice.
[Giordano Luna]

3.3.3 Thrilling Scepters of Love

The pre-code Ahrimanic debutante of phlegm enflames the bone-space of my throat. I have not eaten in days and yet there is a bountiful breakfast that blooms in my gut.
[Peachy]

Flowers grow, and yet fabricated evil reigns over the etheric *pantomimesis* of the god seed. The bark of death catapults the youthful bemusement of the One and only dangling sonic rose. Red, and a form of black that exists only as foam, entices the mist of pheromone laughter. I have loved before but not like this; in time, all will bark with a hydrated smirk: acephalic and left-handed, loaning out a bridge to serve to parted friends.
[Goddess Mia]

Set your life on the table and we can talk. Show me you want me more than you never have not wanted to, and I will love you like no one has, like the zinc-laden pearl in your piebald eyes socket.
[Peachy]

Too many clauses are a kind of mace to the face. Stop it with your lovelorn purple languaging. A peristaltic brigade of bath salts and mind's eyes will take off with your head. Believe it or not. It is up to you. But you would do well to remember the lords and ladies who grift along the Bay. After

the last turn, it all amounts to nothing.
[Elegant Sadie]

If there was a future or a past, I might care about what you say. But I am not sure that even the curvature of spacetime can account for the curveball the Beloved tosses already always at the behest of this desiring-without-an-object, the obsequious castling melancholy of joyful swearing, a Tourette's anthropo-drome for the loosening bells of Time's gagging throat.
[Peachy]

Out in the blastosphere sits a cradle for a youngish pup, a Christic load of tufted grains of froth. You smile at me like the lost river of pearls has once again inundated you with feelings of laughter. This is unbelievable. Love has come here again . . . and we are all in for it Now!
[Fecund Samuel]

This is criminal. But when the clock strikes midnight only thirty-three and a third of all of this will make it to the end of the thread. Ariadne loosen your spool, for the end of days comes not with a stiffened cold, but with an unrestrained divine fire.
[Elegant Sadie]

 *inner parade of massive signs of taperings-off. Fellow*

3.3.4 Burning: An Inverted Romance

I have waited my whole life in vain to find you here, sweet one. I know you are here in my soul and it is a saccharine delight to take you on. For I am but a young miser and I have stocked up on weaponry my whole life. I carry the seed of inversion, too. And I will use it,

every day, every hour, every second, to see you in the flesh.
[Knight Bringer]

Welcome, unholy one. Welcome to my lair.
[Elegant Sadie]

Sweetness. I implore you: come lick my face, O evil one. Come close, for I have a secret to tell you. I have come to lick you back.
[Knight Bringer]

A tiny kingdom of experience is being shadowed by a lack of control. If it is supposed to work like this, it should be honest with the peasants. A strong white lion succumbs to two months of variegated satiety: there are no more toads left to eat, and all the court jesters have been embarrassed back to hell.
[Elegant Sadie]

Wait, wait. There is a situation that must be lived out. There is no emotional openness in the cavalcade; there is no one left to throw off the train. To teach, to build, to implant—these are the workings of the meager. When it happens, it happens faster than it ever has, and so a lot of pain will revel in your energy. A willingness to transcend the bloat will skinny your corpulent tendrils.
[The Forgotten Decanter]

The ontic gets pushed around. How are the bells and whistles of this life? To breathe, to think, to will . . . it takes a level of analysis too broad and too deep to understand. At the heart of the matter sits the eternal sophist posing questions that have no answer. Everything bounces around in tandem with its opposite as if Wolfram alfalfa is growing

at the nave-centers of all non-systematicity.
[**Knight Bringer**]

Flirting with disaster as always, I see. A creation story so rife with blood that the method man's system thinks its own incoherent de-coagulation. There is an army of frostbitten thoughts pervading the moats of disaster. I am burning in hell and I have never loved so deeply in my entire life.
[**Elegant Sadie**]

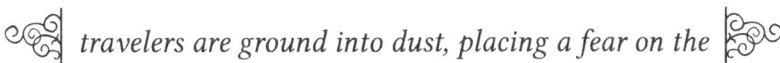 *travelers are ground into dust, placing a fear on the*

3.4   Lack of Response

Material exchanges. It is all done, and the effort has been put in, even though it ended a long time ago. There is no luck in the cup, but a knight of swirls dances feverishly at the cusp of the whipped meringue. Dark energy permeates your face, and bereft of a timestamp the inverse vacuum puffs up the cheeky chemistry of internal conflict.
[Giordano Luna]

With this, I thee give. An intense falling in love with unreality annoys and annuls the post-exit stratagem of compiled futuristic buildings. Obsessive and fawning over a gutter, a small mite leaps over your momentous head. It is about to burst.
[**The Beloved**]

The mite or my head, or in between my molars?
[Giordano Luna]

Neither! There is a mi(gh)ty wind coming from the soul of the mountain and it is bagging up heads. Do you wear your legs crisply or undulated?
[The Beloved]

There was never a choice: undulated. But I doubt that looking within will provide anyone with repose. In my experience, taking inventory of one's organs is useless. One is always missing "this" liver or "that" stomach. Blame it on the vivisectioner, I suppose. Entreated by gloaming entrails, this *"puh"* is the sound of my pin-up head.
[Giordano Luna]

Does it matter no more to you that Moloch is dead and gone?
[Angelfly]

No one suffers here any longer, that is, unless they fail to undergo the inversion. All the mites are slime molds. A head is always a head that floats in its own entrails—nothing but an oven mitt for a beautiful hovering penanggalan.
[Goddess Mia]

Minutiae will not help. Let it be. A list of complaints glides in the maze, and it is a very good time to check in on your *gumby-being*. You are stretched far too thin to make any sense!
[Angelfly]

There is a lot going on in my stomach. I cannot vomit anymore and there is no exit for the lost last king of blood clots. In terms of what is actualized, all I can say is that a dancing femur boasts of its wood-fired grill, upon which the Mage begs for its head in fervour. "I am the Mage," he says. "I am the flute in the song of your unlife. Let me in and peace will come. Do nothing and it will not." The latter is the better choice, *methinks*. If one does not know that for which one asks, one will not receive that which was never asked for: a lack of response is a full-force tallywhacker. Let it go and move on peacefully.
[Giordano Luna]

 *tongue of malaise, pneumo-sending turkey drippings into*

3.4.1   Penance of the Whirligig

If the others try to say important things, the better it all will be. We got stuck in the moon auger and now nothing will sign the contract. It takes 29 degrees of Saturn to frolic in the Bay of Lamentation.
[The Forgotten Decanter]

> So, what does it mean? It all changes size so much that over fifteen hundred creatures light up. I see them come and go all the time. Do not act as if there is nothing of which to be ashamed. The molar indicates that you grind your teeth. *Wherefore art thou?*
> [Giordano Luna]

Discordant aspects form like a non-qualifier. The nodes fester in your lunar heart-sphere. Believing the square-circle to be a lumbering frog was the first and only mistake I have ever made. I will not take penance for the newfound king.
[Elegant Sadie]

There is something funny going on. There is a choice to be made here. It is stagnation or it is fruition: what is represented is not an opportunity or a teleology, it is an influence—and a very strong one at that. Better things will not come as long as an ambition lurks in the throne room. Give it up or forever squeal like a screeching pigboy.
[The Forgotten Decanter]

Do you feel it yet? There is a deep sorrow here, and the moon is transiting your hell. Two times ago, I thought it quite vexing. This time, I find it addressing a matter that I had forgotten about since the unsure musings of youth. A scorpion plucks at the bill of your cap. There is a parade for untimely clinamen, uplifting the barking hammer in your spine!
[Elegant Sadie]

You forget one thing and it is true! When the steamer built this mode, a challenge was accepted: if all were to be as they are, first they must careen the slime of the scum-vapours. We inhale this putrid non-liquidity, the neon airspace of lemon-faced gagging, so that we do not impale the life forces. What has been forgotten, as can be seen by your misplaced *wont extimacy*, the slicing edge of the aural-psychoanalytic meta-transference between yourself and the Mage, is that the spirals never end. The closed system has been opened by the second coming of the changeling—the human—the breather of strands and shapes. He has come back and, boy, are we in for it now . . .
[The Forgotten Decanter]

 the puckering mouths of Neanderthal "kings of the

3.5 Unparalleled Caru-Center

There are poor, intermediate, and rich ways to reach The Opalescence. Whatever you have been told, leave it at the doorway. You have found yourself here, so you also always already have not, and at the end of the crisp leaflet oxidizes the disemboweled reality of the immanent entrails of navel-gazed accordion laughter.
[Goddess Mia]

I hear your huffs, and your puffs, and—Whoa!—you have blown my house off the limit-cliffs. This auto-ethnographic hologram prurience eschews the unreality of the daze, the supplanted gesture towards knighthood, that is, a crypto-currency of mold and danger mites. It is all here, all of it. It never left; it never arrived; it is not, and it is *not* not. Cull the titans. Suck the periwinkle mollusks off my feat, for there is a grandeur birthing from the tips of the unattained mountain top.
[Sigmund Þórisson]

Ladies and Gentlemen, I give you: the candle wrought iron stench of giving's ultimate un-end. Here, on all sides and underneath, atop and inside, Outside, and always within, lurks all the highs and lows of duty's proscription, the magnitude of forged iron dipped in a molten bird bath. Welcome to the goat center of life. Here, we all give way to give all.
[Gypsy Spoon]

Promise the layer of spurl that it will always be this way, that the passing of the torch will not go on in vain, but that, every day, when one must brush off the existential rust of criticism, you intend to give all and nothing but, forever, coming back in a spherical, wintered bane, which, gritty and hopscotch-like, upends the valour of non-human animals and etherites. Today, on this numinous pedestal, spawns a kind of love, an

eternal caru, the care of a mutation-cum-elucidation: the dawning of the first *I without a me*.
[Goddess Mia]

Be that as it may; be not that me I *see*. Whispering and silent, towed to death, drowned out, crowned up, and in a revered steed with a lumbering, if not divine, gait, all the revolting repulsion addicts take their stand against the enemies of the void.
[Fecund Samuel]

It will be a breakdown of epic proportions, in which a slime of Cascadian ice tips will fall out and all over, perpetually, within and without the anarchic redaction of Self. Imbue the effervescence with a stark, violet craftsmanship and the Rainbow of Unhidden Dreams will annul the exacting harbour of unending fire. The end of history will show that three purple hearts erase the limit-experience entirely. First, one must take care of any unattended business with themselves. Then, as always, they are surrendered to the pinnacle of the Seventh Sun.
[Sigmund Þórisson]

Hark, the hominid's posterior sings!
[Gypsy Spoon]

 carnivalesque." Does the flavour of it propel the youth into

Part Four:
Surrendered Pinnacle

a courtly demise? Does the locus of persuasion come at

4.1 Deathbed Made of a Lurching Stampede

You can't even save face in the manger. Wrestling with the face of God, it bears, unknowingly, one hundred thousand facial retirements. The metamorphoses of menialisms corresponds to the withering performances of the first superessential results of the forebearers, those who, in the night of day, crowd out the watchers and the controller, the damned kings whose success depends upon nothing less than a series of communal beheadings.
[Sigmund Þórisson]

Black pyramids: all corrupted. Barking lemurians fated to death, and the wyrd kindred nature of The Twin. The only foreshadowed non-chimerical gut showdown that, in its own lupine millennialism, ensconced the very tip of the cyborg, is in fact floating currently on a seasoned crispy bog.
[Angelfly]

The myriad commercialization of fourth-wave antinomian eventualism takes as its hoarse, crooked prisoner the foaming lamentable exactitude of contingency's malleable un-end. If it once took three barkings, it now takes a fourth—and I never saw the forthright element of proscription unearth the land's tide more than I did in the third year minus Zero.
[Sigmund Þórisson]

Be that as it may, a third maleficence is indeed needed to procure the fourth. Yet, there is a rotting candelabra just in the corner of your resin, one which shapes the coagulant of the mire itself, frothing with two brick buildings and enraptured by a hog's caress. There was a time when the vicissitude of horns flattened out the jury's vestigial, gonadic abeyance, but that time has come and gone, well, fourteen lifetimes from now. If we wish to move forward, then let all that is known to be unknown die on a bed of lemon roses,

for there are a thousand thousand bison grazing as the debutante caresses its own auto-fruiting semi-conduction.
[The Forgotten Decanter]

Because of lag time, then, yes, fine, let all the flavoured drippings be un-banished from below the stares of the yawning ferrymen. A boat floats as hue, and a blue bastard, nimble with flakes for hands, rotates the pickled stupour of "cardinal directions" like a masque and a buried dog borne of a sanctimonious succour. Ouch! Ooooh, it has squandered all the pain again, for fear of suffering wolves who might bite the bark out of this eavesdropped ontology.
[Sigmund Þórisson]

Crispy, rotated again with white rice dripping from eye ducts red with mange. Volatility is not the prelude you endured, neither is the unfurling melodious chords of serpentine, bawling whines. I hear it again—the stark confusion of a lark being a bee—so you better grip this non-existence in the palm of your amnesiac delimitation frenzy. It takes forty-eight more to reach a hundred, and at twelve thousand the number will be reached forever, though with your consent, of course.
[Angelfly]

They will not take it for payment, that is for sure. They never have and they never will. But I heard the truth in the bark that gives, via the incumbent a priori fortitude of a digging grave, its uneven harnessed growl to The Maker, that a kind of hue will thus erupt at dawn. You heard that right: a colour will grow as the dark mistress of delight, a heart transplant of chakric propulsions.
[The Forgotten Decanter]

 the behest of a periwinkle nightingale? Doubtful.

4.1.1 Doubled Liniment Blue

—◆—

It is impossible to enter heaven because one is always already there, ensconced in the immanent waves of fire that name the angels in descending order from nine to One. There is a divinity here that has never entered because it has never left. It spurs on the Grey Gate of Three and impassions the deep, enthralling virtues of blue. In our melancholic bubbling condition, the virtues of regret are operationalized.
[Goddess Mia]

No devices can quell the absence of fire. Anger, hurt, futurity: all spit out a violence that is also a penance. There is no hair shirt in the world that is worth ruining one's kenosis over. For it must be realized that it is not the hair shirt but its privative, analogical expiation that drives the situation of incredible suffering.
[Peachy]

So be it! Affliction looms in the thriving impulses of prudent and paramount gusts of unbearable fluids of time. Impulse this and impulse that . . . no one can see the point of ludic departure, for there is not a wanton crisp of frisky might that could upend the poisoned god. May your medicine strike quickly and sharply. One way or another, the winged submarine always never sinks on the plane of immanence.
[The Beloved]

My pride is boosted when it should be avoided, and yet to be devoid of a friendship or a clan or a doubled liniment blue is the a priori feast for a kingdom running its engine off nothing but the fumes of turquoise envy. Get behind something or nothing will not never come.
[Fecund Samuel]

Be happy for me, that is, unless you cannot undo not undoing but the gossiped silence of a floating manger. I will never try to outdo you or anyone or anything because I am filled to the gills with qualities that garner no rivalry.
[Peachy]

Your arrogance precedes you, eluding my flower tips at the end of the scone.
[Fecund Samuel]

If I came off as competitive, it is only because I indulged in not indulging. This being-in-jest is nothing but a misplaced modifier in the semiotic haze of your draft wizard nincompoop soul-center of blue. When I come back the prophecy will be given, though not by me. That is merely a detail, not a proposition.
[Peachy]

I feel a desire coming on.
[Angelfly]

Yes. There is a compound fracture speeding around the corner of your temperance. Remain prudent!
[Goddess Mia]

 Ouch! We almost forgot to let the wheel out of the cage,

4.1.2 Pleasure Signalization

———◆———

Would it be correct if my fingers, turned up and reaching towards your sliming mouth, started melting while addressing the clarity and positioning of a million one-time auto-recurrences of the same? These are radically nimble ways to incorporate the white, even nimble, soffit and facia of the twig-withering dawn of divine questions. Moving forward quickly, to cull the dump, if you will, an infinitive, an action blessed in purple sand, thrusts into the semiotic twirl of recursion. I can hear the fog. I raked the drones. I know that change is tough, but the cold intuitive platform of your opening immanence seals the deal in perpetuity.
[Fecund Samuel]

Bland towels, marigold foam, negated crazes towards the ebullient threshing of hope. Immediately, the immediacy is known. How could it be criticized. There is a god and it is riling against the tide. It might be foolishness irrupting the dark chamber of partisanship, but when it all comes down to it, the gratings are approved, and the stimulants coagulate in the banal throat of "cultural milieu."
[Maxwell Mountain]

You have me crossing my eyes with your effulgent banter, as if the grassroots movement ever existed at all—come on now! It laughs and sheds its ambiguity upon the aim of operationalized pedantic whispers. Two thousand voices dance in the echo parade. Nothing is promised to anyone, so your god is a quacking seamstress jaunting down to the amnesiac cloud center.
[Sigmund Þórisson]

Souls advanced enough to know that there are three elder spoons which heat the opioid nonchalance of existential magnanimity know, without knowing, that the fourth spoon is a result made purely of the spoon's inexistence. Run that one down the line and let it simmer on the hot box encoffination of a real dominion, of a birch too strong to bend, of a listening, cocked and ready, rightly, to ride the prism of your unfurling fear-eating.
[Maxwell Mountain]

Bogged down, sweating against the tide of perennial swarth-loading, sits, under the Gnome Tree, all of life's frail binges. Who ate the liver? Who killed the chords of peonic glissades, whimpering and wanton as they kicked up a flowering demon of lust? Die with me, always, for this jouissance signals a load too broad to carry, one maxed out, yes, just like a cruising reminder of another lifeless continuance of rigidity.
[Sigmund Þórisson]

This is what it feels like in war. It impales like a smattering of derisional lawless darkness upon the errant, flowing constriction on the shallowing fences of the blood-heat alive in my heart. I do not know when freedom was promised, but this did not turn out like I wanted it to. And I trust that the forty-fourth tablature, a reigning gestalt, will fit itself for the a priori pleasure signalization of my looming resurrection. Up and at it, it was twelve, and then six, and at two it was One.
[Fecund Samuel]

 that turns the screwy downtrodden ventricular past life

4.2 Transnominalist Euphoria Harvest

Monad-like, sucking teeth for Lent, and in the caress of a disharmon(t)ic generator, there exists, like wine, a falling, deep purple, purely nominalist trans-grandeur which calls to us from the Bay. What might the 'call of fools' do for us? In time, we'll see. For now, only the metanymphonic harpsichordian breach slime falling out from your nose can be trusted as the base ointment of your scum anointment. Howling, blistered stones encompass the light field as it fuses its own nuclear generation. Scatter it all, all my whispers in the dark, for the transhumanist un-corruption of flying drones will sever the creeping butch from the mane.
[Maxwell Mountain]

Oh, the old tempest in a teapot, eh? You think you can just send in the troops and all will be handled accordingly, as if the pecking bark of negation has never tasted a candied pinch, never longed for danger, never been abandoned on the chase? Swallow the lemons now, for your ultimate euphoria awaits beyond the Bay. In time, all will be ferreted away in the frenetic dance of mega-chakra imbalance, in a wet, swift dive into the forgotten woods. Gentle, pious, mirth-like: I organized the pumice.
[Elegant Sadie]

So what? When this garden was planted, some fourteen aeons ago, there was nothing there but a troglodyte imagining corpse, sick with worm food, to caress the night in earnest. If it has not come for me yet, then it will never come. And so, I will eat some shit for that nonsense for all time to come. Curl the heart-center. We're taking you home.
[Maxwell Mountain]

It was recommended that when this time came, all the fruitfulness of the gyroscope would be limited to only two hours as experienced by a human being in this solar systemic disease. Hop on, for neither hope nor intention can undo the karmic must of the lust wrapping through the double-helixed drone of the universal humdrum. Not even a sigh can fathom this place any longer.
[Peachy]

What has been planted must now be harvested, this earth, a world, never-becoming and always-lessening the waning death of fork-time, scooped up in the manger of a rotting spoon.
[Maxwell Mountain]

I am the big spoon of Love. You are the little spoon. It has never stopped you before, and it will not begin now. Eat these fowl before they rot.
[Goddess Mia]

Okay, okay. I feel it now. There is a scum-threading series of dots beyond the Wall of Ten; it attends to the passage of time and links in with my perception of the Fair Maiden as the one true queen-beyond-queens. Every single second of suffering has been worth it, just so I could apprehend the undoing of this pain-for-me in favour of *that pain*, which is today, the non-pain of unending desire, a desire without an object, no less.
[Maxwell Mountain]

Who needs ten when there are twenty? And thirty plus three is the answer to a question never posed to a single soul ever in the history of the thirteen aeons. This *eidetic trans-nominalism* trends in the opposite direction, leaving us here as the gerundive slaves of a birthing infinitive.
[Peachy]

It is eight to five hundred, then we are done. It seems as if the time has already passed. We have been harvesting the ecstatic "mulling over" of death, like a pride of lions cricketed and dropped into a bantam loop. Amen!
[Elegant Sadie]

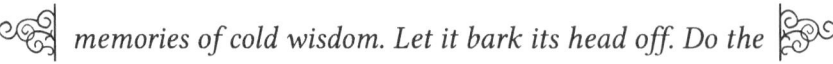 *memories of cold wisdom. Let it bark its head off. Do the*

4.2.1 Bionic Bliss Aggregator

It has two bionic arms, a look upon its face tells ghost stories of fire and ice, and the grave swallows your unending etheric tailbone, the Swedish fish of your bloodborne ineptitude. From without, we will see the visions. From within, the king promises to annul the scant, sun-like forest of attaching legs to worms. Sifting like the blood of time, inching its way forward, as if prayer would tame the white knight's cathexis, you must walk all alone, to take on the netherworld's luminous, kissing monster of faith.
[Chalice Gills]

Who can show me the way? I have prayed for ten thousand days and not once has the Godhead directed me where to go or what to do. Have I sinned too much? Have I donned the halo's breathing axis with less than a one-hundred percent benevolence? Smashing the golden lamp of denigration, I will eat a demon and bewitch the knight of faith, releasing the Goat-One's hold on me.
[Knight Bringer]

Remember: redemption is only as dissolving as it is spasmodic. You have not unnerved yourself enough yet, and so, you will undergo a birth instead of an annulment. To be dead is

easy. To inexi(s)t would be to feed the light, and it is oh so hungry, my friend. Power, glory, reigning glowing bliss. The Evil One knows my steps, hears my growls, and undoes the firmament. What do I care? Nothing is any more important than anything else. And my body withers as I speak this heresy. It pains me; it all really does.
[Chalice Gills]

Open your bowels. Scrunch the tepid meringue of death, you foul-smelling astonished One. The Lord on High wipes His ass like a frown inverts a smile. I laugh and I pray that you never cross hairs with banshee screams, for it will be the end of something—what that is, who cares!
[Knight Bringer]

There is something humming beneath the scalding fire of grease, inside the blemished scone of your forked valley—quaking the Quaalude king out of his shined up and shunned out bootstraps. Do you hear it? It beckons a restoration.
[Peachy]

The Aggregator, yes, it is it who chomps you to bits in succession, in order to prepare its powerlessness and in due time the spirit revival. Do you even know where you are? Have you even the faintest idea what is happening—in this moment, in this quaking valley's shaking bones? I must say, you are even more bewildered than the one who came before you, and he was as lost as a mussel in a popcorn bottle.
[Chalice Gills]

These bionic bits of meatless conundrum, this countenance, the bulbous liquidity of youth . . . I have no idea what is happening. I never have, and I never will. Your reduction of my inexistence-cum-annulment to a veritable "excavation of bewilderment" shall only prove to pave the way for the next one after me. There is a storm brewing. Upon this ferried river, I will forever dunk into my ceaseless headlessness, always and ever-most.
[Knight Bringer]

4.2.2 Gradations of Wolf Hypercubes

There is a wound beyond the crux of the dyad. It is a commonplace error to forget your uprightness, that the horizontal axis of the spine is derivative of the molten rot of Olde. Kiss my feet, you lovelorn selenium junky.
[Elegant Sadie]

Tepid waters crave the wolf. You forget, but it all happened right here, just beyond the backwards reckoning of birth, when the mime corroded the brain of a slug with the magician's hand of doom. They all want to come here to play. And yet, not even one of them is brave enough to stay the night.
[Giordano Luna]

Check the fated hypercube. The wolf stirs. It bends its paws. It feigns its own howl against the mountain range of mirth-death. The next time it sees you will be the last time I ever die. The dead play checkers with your soul as the wolf awaits you just abreast the dark wood's corner.
[Elegant Sadie]

This is the third day in a row that I've just floated here. Do you think we even survived the blood parade? I suppose it is high time for some flavour, but I cannot eat another minx—not now, not ever. Bring the wolf out from its sleep, for now is as good a time as any to sink. The blood mire transposes the lice in my eyes, and all is but a cumrag on the whirligig.
[Gypsy Spoon]

Your penance is seven gradations less than a flat series of wolf hypercubes. Alone and undone is the way we must move forward. I am embarrassed of the temper I once used against the crux of time. The wolf is near and there is not a signal to stop, never the will to fight, and not even the fires of hell will be able to stop it from doing whatever it wants with us.
[Giordano Luna]

The stone is made of clay. If it comes, beat its head with the stone. In it are etched seven riddles. If the wolf bleeds, we will know it instantaneously. If it floats like you and I, then we are in for a hell ride if ever I saw one.
[Gypsy Spoon]

The cake is as sweet as a suffering mannequin, and all the false dummies of the cauldron's heat will roast the fire in fits of luscious threes. A spider, the Godhead, and the weeping Queen Bee herself will avail us the win. Bang your head. Erect the puzzle. The wolf is here! (And its scum-sour lips align directly with the green-gray jaws of lepers' kin!)
[Elegant Sadie]

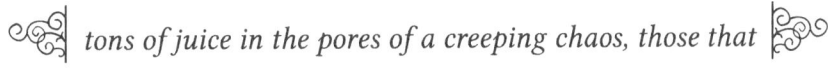 *tons of juice in the pores of a creeping chaos, those that*

4.3   Domed Punctum

Under the swirling moon, it comes back again. It launders the tide with rainbow dirt and reaches out to the seven from the three. There is a great weight releasing from within the dome of your soft lips. Mmmn . . . I cannot decide if to grow is to incise the third day's distortion, rotting as it does so gleefully. A silver bullet might kill the Wolfman, but a delight never to be espoused is the telic victimization of the fires of Hell. It came for you and you are here, so let loose and play a little. It cannot rain within the dome.
[G. W. F. Slagel]

Buzzed, aquatic, a perfect pregnant day for rain. If it cannot rain in here, why does the saliva burn my eyes? In this brainwashed pumpkin patch, the skin, it drips, like a waterway straight to the thirteenth flower. You know, the one that wretches in the spleen. No one, I mean no one, can save the magnet buzzer quaffing bolts for brains. Remember this: a teleportation device is loaded in the anal cavity of tomorrow's yearning. Plug up the ditch or expel its growling nature.

[Giordano Luna]

Coned, longed for, at the limit of starched forensics. Hide the bodhi, stench the blade, for a dreamer spins in the dome. The edge of time sleeps upon the dense corpse of its own leavened bloat-body. Shadows cannot contain. Its appearance is a severed head. The flesh, its meal; it is done, it's over. Delight in it like Socrates' daemon, as there will never be another like me again.

[G. W. F. Slagel]

I hear you. Do you remember the time The Mother quaked the ocean over the tip of your tongue? The tinge of your burnt throat tells a story. I will listen to you speak until the end of time simply because I cannot do otherwise. You do realize that, right? It has a flaw—*all of this*. It believes it is its own heir apparent. But do you not question the digging of this grave? An entire universe was formed, the entire entropy of billions upon billions of years' worth of heat just building upon itself, boiling things to a degree so hot that, after so many illusive samskaras, the being and swallowing of rocks, then plants, then animals, and now you are here, in this ever-present moment talking to me as if a single solitary soul in the post-history of anything ever that was thought, created, made, or forgotten, gives a single shit about it. I have not come here to poke fun but rather to poke a hole in

this ballooning sense of pride in this breathing-that-speaks. Turn around, or else the tide will pull us all into the obsidian abyss.
[Giordano Luna]

The melody plays its sandblasted curmudgeon dirge for October. All things play the river of their *omnipoeisis*, the sprawling chaos of amusical splendors. A quest, an accordion squeezing its ambient fluorescence. Cull the streams. Enter the Ocean.
[Goddess Mia]

A bellhop and a lust for death parade within this manger. The dome was erected for days just like this, and it is high time that we get moving on. An arrow-shaped pyramid is being harvested from your liver. Can you not feel its hidden burling? Slime wafts in the wet dust of time. Snowbirds drift on the sliding white ice of the twin castles' double-barreled motes. In one hundred and twelve years, ninety-three will become ninety. I can feel it. It punctures my soul and softens the impression. A feeling has arisen in the domed happenstance quaffing non-chalance, the lethargy of "life." Seven it is. Four. Three. Two. One.
[G. W. F. Slagel]

Sixty. You were right. Sloping, it turns its head. A dime, a pulpit, a crispy leathered twinkling eye. The sun is rising and yet here we sit. It is nice to talk but we ought to move. Let's shake off the old tombstone and crawl out. I've got no shovel, but I've got two hands. And it is getting hard to breathe.
[Giordano Luna]

 the sea, wish to make up for their undesirous travelcards?

4.4 Black Crow is a Spinning Black Hole

Smile at the target, the world is waiting behind the soft dripping malaise of reprehension. Like a wound which, in a gluttonous moment of pride, closes itself for fear of its expanse, the blue sprawling corpse is lifted from our grave. Breathing like the toned-down façade of several lives lived at once, as if the grandeur of a life is imparted by its living out and not its failure, the pig of mirth walks over to point the way. Heavy, dripping of droppings of corticosteroid-infused lipids, lab mice, and fats, the sun rises. Golden domes, pyramidic self-escape routes, and the third thought of the morning coalesce: the big black crow is finally here. It has come to open us to the Gate.
[Gypsy Spoon]

> The mutation has spiked. The big black crow of nine is at it again. There is a loss of acquiescence and the gallstone is wedged between my teeth. I cannot find my brain and there is a soul that wraps around the plank of your pirated immanence.
> [The Forgotten Decanter]

Granted, it takes a while to feel it. To be within the immanent caress of Love's behest is to note clearly the fecund second nature of the dyad's preponderance. Say it clearly: "two stones roll down the hill of quaffed spectrality." The third stone is right between your eyes, victimizing you towards your utter maddening lifeline to heaven.
[Gypsy Spoon]

> Yawning morality plays eat their own flatulent rigor mortis. Wet actors surf the low tide of lawlessness, spinning in the gypsy dance and surmounting a cry. There is no director here. Do you understand? No one is in charge. You've lost your head. And not even the acephalic breath of the universal scream will be tender enough to pack up the bags under your eyes.
> [G. W. F. Slagel]

Crow the rod, lighten the feather, for all is well in the land of the blue tangerine swallowing the gust of its misty flower. The blood king called upon the wanton sleep cradle over eleven times in one morning as he reached, in delighting over the undoing of his craw-liver, the most infernal of planes, cawing the black crow suffering itself in a spinning black hole of your destroying purulence. Valiant, yes, but upon the tip of your tongue even a moon wretch can dance without a saddle. And you know *exactly* what I mean.
[Sigmund Þórisson]

Look up. Do you note the strange pink loop in the unstained cloud of might? See in it your reflection before the hole takes off. We've been spinning since before the first whisper and the angels drift towards us without firmament, filling, or even a crippled series of downed wires. It is because of lead that our feet drag. In the moat, right before the curious feebler upends its illicit namesake, is where sound will be all but drowned out. And then, the fifteenth twin will make its way to the opened door. A vivisection is a drought of mental catastrophic fits.
[G. W. F. Slagel]

 It took the penny-pinching lives of death to get us here.

4.5 Spacetime Dent Suction

Let it draw in the mud. A skull haven, ribbing for a jab, well, that is who will awaken. For all this time, we thought that the fig was laced with cement. How harsh it is to come to realize the hard, cool death of the flock.
[Fecund Samuel]

The cloaked nomad is in danger. It is a real mess if I say so myself. Not even a slammed dent in time will resurrect the marsh now, not even a slab of bacon will kill the rite of the inverse hydrocladia. Burl these branches back into disease. Only vomit clones the dust of your mitigating youthful smile.
[The Forgotten Decanter]

You give it all to the dent wherein we stop, but the true test of space is its glittering, damning obsolescence. Enroll in the new class. We are here for the death of God. Every flavour on this cavalcading prurience shall lick the face of angelic revelry. A pink casket awaits the tripled tongue of slicing cheeks.
[Maxwell Mountain]

Shop the spiced tree atop the Vienna sausage of super-crawling benefaction. Maple tongued scum. All of it. Hardly a day goes by that is not in error of its own negation. Prized are the thinning trees, the stapled heads, the weening pods of *hologram xenoglamour*. Lift your shitting heart, for the Pleiadean skirts of time are running amok in this forever-denting spacetime fabulation.
[Peachy]

This is nothing more than a furled river for a poetics of the staunch grey goat, the whole non-gradient barn for a writing *outside of the times*. Haven't you heard of the rife conundrum of the burly blade? It cuts off the soiled head for nothing but a ragged edge of fumbling words, leaning against the fraught drought of a skim theory of "unlife and dearth."
[Angelfly]

A semiotic skull cap full of skill and lacking in ever-ready deeds of malnourished flesh. A puppet dances in the dark. Over there. You've seen it out your eyes for days and yet a flock of peppered wasps bites the hands that feed. We've got

one last shot. Let us party like it's nine nine nine.
[Gypsy Spoon]

 Suckling toads, both corroded and benign, begin to hunch.

4.5.1 Glittered YHWH Triage

Below the whacked suffrage of marigold whims—a personage nevertheless abreast the capped audial consequences of the battles that were won—sits the genuflected harp of my beloved's godly impropriety, prioritized by its very gobsmacked anti-propertied godheadedness. I am a slain warrior coming into the remainder of the Christ. Here sits the bamboozled cusps of bolting a breath to the wind.
[Giordano Luna]

Bearing down on the fire one can only ever sit at the bonehead, quaking firefly fistfuls of godhead and thus bemoaning the plain white snake of Three. You have made it this far and, although wounded, let it be and let it be known that the truth of a warrior's sheen is only ever as stout as it is meringued. Long ago, the kindred stamp of flesh was defined by its porous veracity. These days, one must barrel down for triage. There are forty beds but only one pillow, which, billowing down on the cradle of your youth, welcomes, entranced, the last full measure of your crispy deeds.
[Goddess Mia]

Have no fear, for the setting Sun has heard no whisper that would take Mine grace from you. You live your life like a swan caressing the Mage, and in buttressed fermenting Love shall I swallow you whole. I eat always and everywhere to give you life. Everything is always exploding and there is no place to hide. Sleepless nights are the eternal, pink-shorn haze of darkness collapsing upon the destination of your Heart.
[The Beloved]

It comes to rule for Everything. The battle is lost, can't you see? It is so right, and I am not on the right side of sanctimony. I am not even not that. Look, it hurts to live in pain, but the conservative nature of lye is in the way its spiders reveal the napkin drawer, peeling wet, drooling whimpers out of your futile mind-body knapsack. Full, flown in, curbing around the edge: here we go again with all the triages. If it lives, let it be. If not, do not not let it. *Sheesh.*
[Knight Bringer]

A worm scratching its tooth for seven drawers of tigres de papier. All slain, all day. No one has ever loved me like You do. There is no luck, no escape, from this Love. I am making fifty-thousand mistakes a minute and you still caress my mule-bowing heat. I am the king of Hell and eat muskrats out of draining wounds, and not for one single second did you doubt my exuberant gyrating immanence. I do not deserve any of this. *Take me home.*
[G. W. F. Slagel]

It rides again, it rides the kumquat for spinning mountains. There is glitter falling from the patch of mulberry trees frowning out of your eyelids. When I was made, there was a single crucifix on the wall. Now there are seventy-two, each mating with the blood eagles of Time. In the distance, a piano plays the soft dirge for the eighth grey moon. I feel the end is near. The end is here and what have we got to say for ourselves? What have we to show for all this? Some semiotic

absurd parading of sticks and wheat, nothing but a pen telling its saviour to curl the glittered gateway to the third tripling moon beyond all-tigers' sins. I am spooked and I have heard the name a thousand million times. Eat of the glittered bane of mankind, for YHWH opens the breast of the floundered ever-pawning *dove-in-itself.* Flying a Way to me, a bed-wetting drifter found God in the furtive glance of a rotting young lamb.
[Sigmund Þórisson]

A poetry of reddish stars longing for the wilting throne of glib discerning whales, each thinking with the spinning dome of glittered pagan moons. Nursing at ground zero, it gives, and it takes away. I am in love with everything ever and its opposite, and, in the dark simplicity of a word choking on its own mouth, all will hear the words and tiptoe back into being. A being-in-Love.
[The Beloved]

Alleluia!
[Giordano Luna] [G. W. F. Slagel] [Goddess Mia]
[Knight Bringer] [Sigmund Þórisson]

 Enhance the flavour mold by doing one nice thing a day,

Appendix:
(Virtual Apoplectic Sponge-culls)

swelling up, around the horns, twos gleam in bullet

-1.-2 Agoraphobics of the Undesired

There is a culture for that—a culture with no mechanizations, one which engineers its own solar funambulism. The bear. The bear is here, and it cannot incorporate you into its spectrum. Around the corner, you will notice a cavalcading series of right triangles, each cubed at the horizon of a clawing spunk. The geometry here is enshrouded in a bear. When it moves left, the sharp center of our world is concussed to the right, severing the light, and putting all our gravity on the shadow at the door. When the bear sits, we buoy back to center, but then the flower is touched, and it sets off a series of motivating factors for the sun's rays to create a taxing cut into the perpendicular slime molds that grow behind the façade. It was once transparent, but it is limited and feels crowded like a funeral parlour, but without all the communal self-blaming. As I've said, the bear pays no mind to us, for it knows nothing of our existence. It is largely true that we do not exist over there, but if the Gilded Age taught us one thing it is that one can do a good job, a very good job, and no one may pay it any mind. There is a hungry bear right behind this room. If it gives you pause, then know that the only reason this happened is because it did not. Wrap your fries around that, Jack.
[Galldust]

 points. Regurgitate wires through the electrical chamber

-1.-1 Basilic Vein Calculus

Far from tapping the veins of a buxom tyrant, the onus of flair, directed at the purple firmament, digs into the mucosal yellowing underground of life. Five seconds of your hymnal time is all it takes to abscond the grain hamper, that tall, inverted silo of short tempers and long tongues. There are excessive priorities and then there are prudent banalities, both of which point beyond the marmalade belch of a tipsy jar of wanton *longing-for-God*. If you feel fooled, take my advice, and open your eyes. The jaundiced circle of Love is radiating and free from any kind of trifling weed-eating, so if, at the very last moment, the circle squares itself,

then you will be able to merge with the ditch, a dirtied and baffling juxtaposition if there ever was one (and there never has been). Cacophony, flutes *playing-with* the noise, as if it were the strangest pinpointing closeness, irony lays in bed with reason, feeling for grace and getting only a stubbing. As a pair of scissors, it cuts the drift. Shearing the mountain, it defends the oracle. Pinpointed and stepping over a marly bridge, the flop is granted. Upright, uptight, filled to the gills and longing, ever so mightily, that the sword of pain will never meet them again, the glee team has funked the river with their own twilight of the gods, infinitesimally.
[Etherite 34587]

 of crispy, tenderloin abscondo-behemoth filters, lemonade

-.1.0 Spore Cauls

Usurp the ghost. Crawling out of the banal crosshairs of a weeping crystalline slime, the dark dead river behind the winding *creatura* winds its liquid eyes up and down the mystical body of undeath. Do not forget that the "impulse to creativity" is but the toned-down lament of a falling bastion of hearth bread tigers, igneous galls of fire that feed upon the fulcrum of indecision. Eviscerate the river to ferment its bloodlust as a pearly gate, the nothing-sphere whose own cradling wafer pageantry will ring the bells of hell. Dispersive being waits in the shallows between the volcanic edge of time and the earthly hollowness of space. It hid behind the shadows as a pale white grimace and, in turn, your face has abandoned the *sapientist nonchalance* of a new and birthing monstrosity: the spore caul of a defunct fungi passing as a posthuman form of breathing.
[Frost Crawler]

 gasping schemata baked as a dish at the end of a parade.

0.0 Fluidic Dispersion Cult

I address you all as if you are lower than scum, but who is it that turned the page?—the lemming or the goat of death? You go *squeee!* with the pigeon tail as if there is something inside you that demands the day. Let me tell you something, folks, there is not a dog in heat that would lick the folic lice off your limey fingers, never a day in the a-phallogocentric history of the un-inverse that would put us on par with "you know who," so why even go there? Take the drip, false the slip, and focus on the Bay. *In the sleep, there is a weak, a weak and tender slay. Beyond the tongue, within the One, and at the cusp of the solid storm—is a dart with the urge of a dream.* Close your eyes and think about the destruction of the separated brick houses, the ones you passed in your youth. Running and hiding is all that is worth this penultimate death. The un-i(n)-verse awaits, *in toto*.

[Angelfly 2.0]

 *Enhance flowers. Earn a decree in slime-shining.*

Fin